Hairy, Hairy Poodle

by Marilyn Singer • illustrated by Abigail Tompkins

Ready-to-Read

Simon Spotlight

New York   London   Toronto   Sydney   New Delhi

SIMON SPOTLIGHT
An imprint of Simon & Schuster Children's Publishing Division
1230 Avenue of the Americas, New York, New York 10020
This Simon Spotlight edition May 2022
Text copyright © 2022 by Marilyn Singer
Illustrations copyright © 2022 by Abigail Tompkins
All rights reserved, including the right of reproduction in whole or
in part in any form.
SIMON SPOTLIGHT, READY-TO-READ, and colophon are registered
trademarks of Simon & Schuster, Inc.
For information about special discounts for bulk purchases,
please contact Simon & Schuster Special Sales at 1-866-506-1949 or
business@simonandschuster.com.
Manufactured in the United States of America 0322 LAK
10 9 8 7 6 5 4 3 2 1
This book has been cataloged by the Library of Congress.
ISBN 978-1-5344-9959-1 (hc)
ISBN 978-1-5344-9958-4 (pbk)
ISBN 978-1-5344-9960-7 (ebook)

There is a dog
that you might meet
in the country,
on the street.

Her coat can simply
not be beat.
No other canine
can compete.

Call it fur, call it hair.

Folks who see her
stop and stare.

She does not molt,
she does not shed.

She does not care
what is on her head. . . .

Poodle coming,
Poodle going.

Poodle's curly hair
is growing.

In sunlight, rain, or
big wind blowing,

Poodle's hair
is always growing.

Polka-dotted when it is snowing,

Poodle's hair keeps
right on growing.

Poodle brings a
ball for throwing,

does not know her
hair is growing.

Poodle in a
boat goes rowing,

does not care her
hair is growing.

Will it stop soon?
Is it slowing?

Nope. Poodle's hair just keeps on growing.

Poodle's eyes are
hardly showing.

Like the grass,
that dog needs mowing!

What is inside there,
tippy-toeing?
Hiding where that
hair is growing?

Look! Two other
eyes a-glowing,
roosting where that
hair is growing.

Uh-oh, do you
hear them crowing?

Are those NUTS that
pair is stowing?

Are those trees that
they are sowing?

Goodness gracious, shoo, get going!

Time for Poodle
to look neat!
Shampoo for you,
rinse, repeat!

Haircut from her
head to feet!
Good girl, now she
gets a treat!

Such nice short curls,
not overflowing!

But right away,
and every day,
Poodle's hair is
always growing.